The Colorless Sara Short

S. Michael Smith — Art by Nathalie Kranich

This is a work of fiction. Names, characters, places, and incidents either are the product of the author's imagination or are used fictitiously. Any resemblance to actual persons, living or dead, events, or locales is entirely coincidental.

Copyright © 2024 by S. Michael Smith

All rights reserved. No part of this book may be reproduced or used in any manner without written permission of the copyright owner except for the use of quotations in a book review. For more information, address: author@author.com.

First paperback edition June 2024

Edited by Glenys Nellist
Book design by Veronica Scott
Illustrations by Nathalie Kranich

ISBN: 978-1-964475-02-8 (hardcover)
ISBN: 978-1-964475-00-4 (paperback)
ISBN: 978-1-964475-01-1 (ebook)

This book is dedicated to my mom.
Thank you for teaching me to dream and reassuring me
that it is sometimes good to live with your head in the clouds.
All of my life I have felt no mountain is too high,
no river too wide, and no dream is out of reach.

Thank you,
Love, Your Son

A butterfly's wings convey fancy things,
Except if you're poor Sara Short.
She sat in the corner all by herself,
Typing the daily report.

The **BUTTERFLIES** lived in the hollow oak tree,
Close to the ground filled with flowers.
They managed each blossom, made sure they were lovely,
Enhancing the warm springtime showers.

Queen Nyla Neat gave out the chores
That needed a butterfly's care ...

To decorate nature, take care of the forest
And GLITTER the warm morning air.

The chores all needed color and grace,
And Sara was lacking in each.

Her wings had no color, and she was too clumsy
Which put those chores way out of reach.

Now The Queen Butterfly loved Sara Short,

And each day she'd have her assist,

To organize goals and help keep things straight,

And care for the springtime chores list.

Sara worked **HARD** to make
The Queen proud,

She'd dream
OF FLOWERS AND SPRING.

She wanted to prove what
she could achieve

In spite of her
colorless wings.

From when she was born,
Sara Short's wings

Lacked the color that
all her friends had.

Her own outward beauty,
if you should ask her,

Was not very pretty, but sad.

The others would tease and point at her wings,

She felt like she didn't belong.

It made her feel different, a little alone,

So Sara learned how to be strong.

Sara worked hard and
did all her chores,

Hoping that her time was near,

When The Queen would
let Sara Short help

TO GLITTER THE WIND

with her peers.

The Queen told Sara that
glitter was nice,

But only one part of the dream.

Day in and day out,
to keep it all working

The hard stuff goes
mostly unseen.

So sadly, for Sara, her time wouldn't come,
As day after day would go by.
She kept helping The Queen to run everything
And tried VERY HARD not to cry.

A FEW YEARS PASSED BY, and Sara Short grew
To become a STRONG butterfly.
Sara felt happy completing her part,
But some days she'd still wonder why.

"Why was I born with colorless wings?
I wish I just simply belonged."
But still, she continued to keep her head up,
And made sure her flutter stayed strong.

Then came the day the butterflies feared,

An hour they all knew would come.
But even though they'd dreaded that day,
It came as a big shock to some.

The Queen had entered the last DAYS OF LIFE,
Her wings were now wrinkled and old.
She'd lived a great life as queen butterfly,
Watching each springtime unfold.

The butterflies worried and
made such a fuss,
For none of them knew what to do.
They relied on direction from their leader each spring,
To make sure the MAGIC'S on cue.

Think of the roses,
the white daffodils,
The BEAUTY of all nature's flowers.
The forest relied on the butterflies' work
To enhance all the springtime rain showers.

And seeing that Sara knew
The Queen so well,

Better than all of the rest,

They begged her to go to their

KINGDOM'S GREAT ROOM

And see what their Queen would suggest.

Sara Short entered the room
of The Queen,

Where there she lay tired in bed.

Sara walked up with
tears in her eyes,

As The Queen held
one piece of THREAD.

"Sara, our lives are like this frail thread,
Searching for where to belong.
It's thin and fragile, and so very short,
But with many threads it becomes STRONG."
"With each passing year some threads become frayed,

The time comes that they are replaced.
And such is my LIFE, like this damaged thread,
Another piece must take my place."

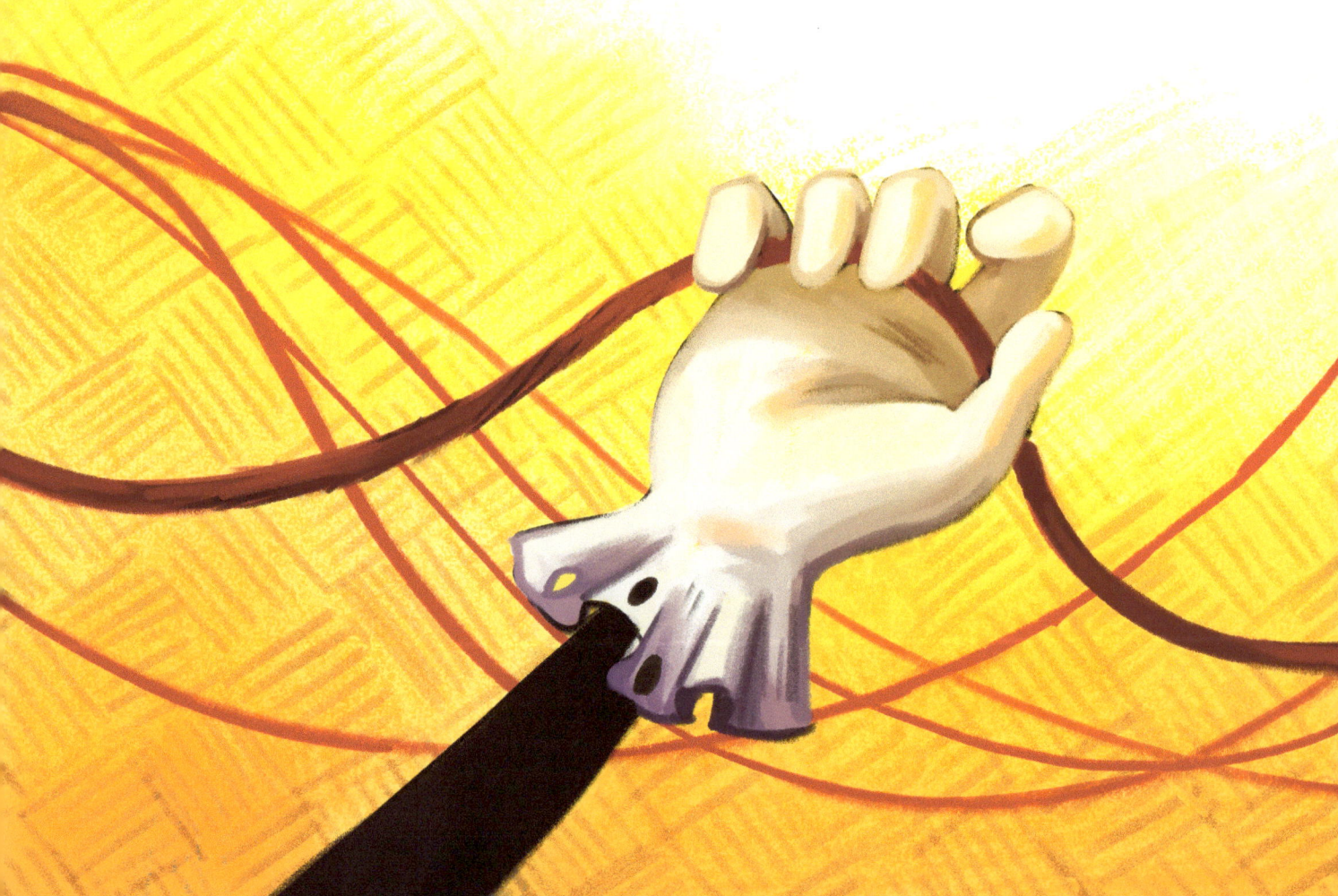

The Queen said softly, "Listen, my child,
For YOU are the key to it all.
You've been by my side year after year,
IT'S TIME FOR YOU TO STAND TALL."

"You know how to rule our sweet butterflies,
You know the true secrets of wind.
You know how to DECORATE all of creation,
The magic lies right here within."

"So go now, my Sara, and please take my place...
Lead with compassion and love.
Attend to the wonders of what's been created,
I'll be watching you close from above."

Sara stepped back and took a deep breath,
She LOOKED AT HERSELF in the mirror.
Sara had never noticed before,
But now it was all getting clearer.

Her colorless wings were always the thing
That kept her from finding her place.

But now, with the blessings of The Queen,
She saw their TRUE BEAUTY and grace.

She spread out her wings in the great kingdom room,
And yes, they both had no color,
But POWER and ELEGANCE shone from the pair
With patterns possessed by no other.

And two final things that The Queen had left...

The first was the butterfly CROWN.
Sara Short smiled and put it on,
Along with the queen's royal gown.

And Sara did just as The Queen had asked,
She led with such GRACE in her court.
And never was there a ruler more loved...

Than the colorless queen,
SARA SHORT.

Printed in the USA
CPSIA information can be obtained
at www.ICGtesting.com
LVHW070713180724
785746LV00006B/94